Caddie
the
Golf Dog

For Jonathan and Joshua —M.S. & B. M. Jr

For Bill and Mike —F. C.

═══════

First published in the United States of America in 2002 by
Walker Publishing Company, Inc.

Published simultaneously in Canada by Fitzhenry and Whiteside, Markham, Ontario L3R 4T8

For information about permission to reproduce selections from
this book, write to Permissions, Walker & Company,
435 Hudson Street, New York, New York 10014

Library of Congress Cataloging-in-Publication Data
Sampson, Michael
Caddie, the golf dog / Michael Sampson and Bill Martin Jr [sic] ; illustrations by Floyd Cooper.
p. cm.
Summary: A stray dog must chose between the first girl who took her in and the two
brothers who gave her a home and helped her care for her new puppies.
ISBN 0-8027-8817-3 -- ISBN 0-8027-8818-1
[1. Australian cattle dog--Fiction. 2. Dogs--Fiction.] I. Martin, Bill. II.
Cooper, Floyd, ill. III. Title.

PZ7.M356773 Cad 2002
[E]--dc21   2002071351

The artist applied kneaded erasers to mixed media on Bainbridge Board to create the illustrations for this book.

Book design by Victoria Allen

Visit Walker & Company's Web site at www.walkerbooks.com

Printed in Hong Kong

2 4 6 8 10 9 7 5 3 1

Caddie
the
Golf Dog

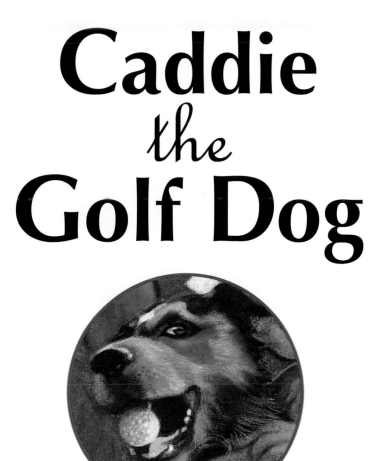

Michael Sampson *and* Bill Martin Jr

Illustrations by Floyd Cooper

Walker & Company
New York

Jennifer cradled the dog in her arms and cried softly. Her dad had warned her that she couldn't keep the stray that had shown up on their doorstep. But for the past few days, Diamond had been her best friend.

"We don't have enough room for a dog, sweetheart," her dad said. "Tomorrow we'll find her a home."

Jennifer held Diamond tightly in her arms, petting her and tracing the diamond on her forehead with her finger. As she put the dog in the backyard for the night, she said, "Have a good night, Diamond. I'll see you in the morning!"

That night a terrible storm came. Thunder crashed, lightning flashed, and Diamond ran around the yard, barking loudly.

Suddenly, there was an explosion as lightning struck the big tree in the backyard. As the tree fell, it knocked the back fence down. And off Diamond ran, her heart pounding and her feet churning.

By the time morning came, the storm had ended. Diamond had stopped running, but all the houses were strange new ones. She didn't know how to make her way back to Jennifer.

Diamond was lost again, and all alone.

Cold, wet, and hungry, Diamond traveled down the road. The town turned into the country, and soon Diamond came to a golf course.

The course was beautiful, with rolling hills of green grass, trees, white sand, and blue lakes. Diamond roamed the course, searching for a friendly face.

Near the sixth tee, Diamond saw two boys in a golf cart. And they saw her.

"Look, Jon. A dog!" shouted Josh. And Diamond jumped into the golf cart with the boys.

The boys' father turned from his shot when he heard the boys' laughter. "Shh," he said, "I'm trying to concentrate."

Mr. Tyler couldn't believe his eyes when he saw Diamond, with her tongue hanging out, sitting between the boys in the cart. "Well," he said, "it looks like you have a friend."

And they did. At every hole Diamond jumped out of the cart, watched the boys hit their shots, and ran to show them where their balls landed. And sometimes she even brought the ball back to them. The boys named her Caddie, because she helped them with every shot, just like a golf caddie would. Now Diamond had a new name.

Finally, at the sixteenth hole, Josh asked, "Dad, can we keep Caddie? She's a great dog!"

"Oh, boys. We are too busy to take care of a dog," Dad said. "Besides, she's too friendly to be homeless. I'm sure she has a family who loves her."

Caddie whined, and the sad sound told the boys that their dad was wrong.

The boys played more and more slowly, but soon they were at the eighteenth hole and it was time to go home. The boys hugged Caddie as they begged their dad, "Please, let's take her home."

Finally, Dad agreed to ask the lady who ran the pro shop about Caddie.

"I'm sure she's a stray," the lady said. "People are always dropping animals off here. But leave your name and number. I'll call you if no one claims her."

As they were getting into their car, Josh whispered, "Stay here, Caddie. We'll be back for you tomorrow."

At home, the boys talked and talked about Caddie. They talked about when she found the lost ball. They talked about how smart she was. And they talked about the way she wiggled every time a kind word was said to her. Neither boy knew what kind of dog Caddie was.

"She looks like a German shepherd," Jon said.

"But German shepherds don't have blue eyes and gray specks on their coats," said Josh.

"Hey, I know how we can settle this," Jon said. "Let's go online and see if we can find a dog that looks like Caddie." So the boys did an Internet search and learned that Caddie was a blue heeler dog.

Early the next morning, the Tylers' phone rang. It was the lady from the golf course. "That dog barked all night long. As far as I'm concerned, she's yours. Please come and take her away!"

And so they did.

Caddie loved her new home and all the attention she received.

It was a happy, busy day. Caddie had to visit the veterinarian, dog food had to be bought, a bed had to be made, and she had to be bathed. That night Caddie slept well, with her stomach full of food. It had been a wonderful day.

During the next few weeks, Caddie became part of the Tyler family. She ran through the woods with the boys. She swam in the pond. She brought the paper to the front door each morning. Every Saturday, she played golf with the boys. But despite all the exercise, she started to grow fat.

One Friday afternoon, Jon discovered that Caddie was gone. Jon and Josh called and called her name, but she did not return. The boys searched everywhere—through the woods, down the road, and even at the golf course. But Caddie was nowhere to be found.

That night two sad and lonely boys worried about their dog. Was she afraid? Was she hungry?

When morning came there was still no sign of Caddie. It was Saturday, but the boys could not bear to go golfing without Caddie. Instead, they searched the woods again.

As the boys approached a big, hollow oak tree, they heard a whining sound. "Here Caddie, here Caddie!" they called. Inside the hole they found Caddie and five healthy puppies. One even had a diamond on her forehead, just like Caddie.

Josh and Jon moved the puppies back to the house and did their best to help Caddie take care of them. A bed of quilts was prepared in the corner of the garage, and Caddie was given all the food she could eat.

In about a week the puppies opened their eyes. Soon they were walking. And two weeks later the trouble began! The puppies loved to chew, and chew they did. They chewed up one of Jon's shirts. They chewed up Josh's baseball glove. And one day Mr. Tyler found his golf shoes in the driveway, all chewed up!

In spite of this, the boys loved the puppies. And the puppies loved the boys.

When Caddie's puppies were six weeks old, Mr. Tyler placed an ad in the newspaper offering them for free.

That Saturday the boys didn't play golf with their father. They stayed at home to see who would come to adopt the puppies. Four families came, and each family took a puppy home with them. The boys were both sad and happy—sad to tell the puppies good-bye but happy the puppies were going to good homes. Now, only one puppy remained—the little one with a diamond on her forehead.

That night, when the boys said their prayers, they prayed, "Dear God, please let Caddie's last puppy find a good home."

On the other side of town, Jennifer's dad called her into the living room. He had the newspaper in his hand. "Jenny," he said, "I am sorry about Diamond. I should have let her stay in the house the night of the storm. I don't know how to say this, but I made a big mistake. Will you forgive me?"

Jennifer answered him with a big hug and a happy smile.

"I know that we can never replace Diamond, Jenny, but would you like a puppy?"

Jennifer squealed as she grabbed the paper. She couldn't believe her eyes when she read: FREE BLUE HEELER PUPPIES.

She rushed to the telephone. Her voice trembling, she asked, "Do you have any puppies left?"

"One," said a boy on the other end of the line.

"Hooray!" shouted Jennifer. "We'll be right there!"

Thirty minutes later Jennifer and her dad arrived. And there stood Caddie and her puppy. Jennifer couldn't believe her eyes. Could this be Diamond? But there was no hesitation from Caddie, who greeted Jennifer with a happy bark and wet licks. Caddie's puppy licked Jennifer, too.

The two families talked about how the boys had found Diamond and why they named her Caddie. Then they talked about where she should live.

"We must ask Caddie," said Jon. "She should decide where she will live."

Jennifer stood at one side of the yard and called, "Here Diamond! Here Diamond!" And Josh and Jon stood on the other side of the yard and called, "Here Caddie! Here Caddie!"

For one second, Caddie did not know what to do. Then she started to remember. She remembered running through the woods with the boys. She remembered the tree where her puppies had been born. She remembered all the adventures and fun she'd had at the Tylers' house and the love Josh and Jon had shown her. She trotted over to the boys.

Jennifer watched in dismay as her Diamond—now Caddie—walked away. But then she felt a wet tongue licking her ankle. She looked down to see a little puppy with a diamond on her forehead looking up at her with deep blue eyes.

With joy in her heart, Jennifer picked up the puppy and said, "Hi, Diamond. It's time for us to go home."